D1417505

Weekly Reader Children's Book Club presents

THE BEAR'S WATER PICNIC

By John Yeoman · Illustrated by Quentin Blake

THE MACMILLAN COMPANY

One fine day in spring, the pig, the squirrel, the hedgehog and the hen, all looking very smart, were making their way to the big lake at the edge of the forest. The hen had carefully preened her feathers, the squirrel had fluffed up her beautiful tail, the hedgehog had polished his spines, and the pig was looking especially pink and shiny.

"Hurry up," said the pig. "We mustn't be late for the bear's water picnic." And when they reached the water, there was the bear, with a large picnic basket and two straw hats. "It's just the day for a water picnic," he called, as they ran up to him. And he gave the pig one of the straw hats.

After they had all said hello to each other, the bear showed them his special surprise—a raft he had made. "Let's float out into the middle of the lake and have a nice quiet picnic in the sun," he said.

Everyone was delighted. They all settled down comfortably on the raft, and the bear gently pushed them away from the shore with a long pole. And away went the raft, gliding smoothly over the blue water between the dark green lily pads.

Soon they reached the middle of the lake. "Just the place for a picnic," the bear said, lifting the lid of the basket.

There was something for everyone:

acorns for the pig,

barley for the hen,

hazel nuts for the squirrel,

dead beetles for the hedgehog

and honeycomb for himself.

What's more, they all had a napkin
with their initial on it to tie around their necks.

But no sooner had they started to eat their delicious
picnic than they heard a loud croaking noise.

"Awrk, awrk," it went. They put down their food and
looked over the side of the raft. And there, on a lily pad,
was a fat frog. "Awrk, awrk," he went again.

"What a terrible noise," said the pig. "He'll spoil our
water picnic if he goes on like that."

But that wasn't the worst of it. The hen pointed her wing at all the other lily pads. There was a frog sitting on each one, and they all started to go "awrk, awrk."

"What a lovely day for a water picnic, awrk, awrk," they said. "May we join you?"

The bear carefully picked up the fat frog and held him on his paw. "We'd very much like to share our picnic with you," he said, "if only you would stop going awrk, awrk." "We can't, awrk, awrk," said the frog cheerfully. "In that case," said the bear with a sigh, "I think we shall have to move on to a quieter part of the lake."

The bear put the frog back on his lily pad, they packed up the hamper and set off again, leaving the noisy frogs behind. They floated across the blue lake until suddenly— without any warning–there was a great bump, and they all fell over on their backs with their legs in the air.

The animals quickly picked themselves up and peered over the edges of the raft to see what had happened. "We're stuck!" wailed the hedgehog. "We've hit a sandbank," said the pig, solemnly.

Their first thought was to get the raft moving again. The hedgehog, the squirrel, the pig and the bear took hold of the pole and pushed with all their might against the sandbank. The hen stood on the bear's head and shouted encouragement. "Push!" she squawked. "Push! push!" But the raft wouldn't budge.

The pig sat down and fanned himself with his
hat. "We shall have to stay here until we are rescued,"
said the hen. "That might be hours," said the squirrel.
"We might run out of food," sobbed the pig. And they
all sat down, looking tired and miserable.

But the bear had an idea. "One of us must swim to the shore for help," he said brightly. But the shore was a long way away, and when they tried the water it was cold and deep. So the hedgehog rolled up into a ball, the hen put her head under her wing, and the squirrel curled up inside the picnic basket. The pig looked embarrassed and said, "Pigs can't swim." "Like bears," said the bear, not quite truthfully.

Then the bear had another idea. "Perhaps the frogs will help us," he said. So they stood up and called for the frogs at the tops of their voices. And soon the cheerful frogs began to appear, awrk-awrking as they came. The animals all started to explain at once what had happened.

"That's easy, awrk, awrk," said the fat frog, and all the frogs began to clamber onto the sandbank.

At a sign from the fat frog they all jumped into the water and made an enormous wave which lifted the raft away from the bank. "We're moving," shouted the animals happily. "Awrk, awrk," croaked the frogs.

As the raft drifted along the grateful animals unpacked the hamper and offered to share their picnic food with the frogs. "No thank you very much," said the fat frog. "You see, your honeycomb attracts flies, and frogs like flies better than anything." And all the frogs' tongues shot out to catch the flies.

After the animals had eaten enough food and the frogs had caught enough flies, the frogs began to sing their "awrk, awrk" song again. But this time the animals were so happy that they joined in: the hen clucked, the hedgehog wheezed, the squirrel chattered, the pig snorted and the bear boomed. They were enjoying themselves.

As the sun began to set over the lake, the five animals and their frog friends drifted to the shore. "Time to go home," said the bear, yawning contentedly, and they all said good-by to each other.

"Come back soon for another water picnic, awrk, awrk," called the frogs.

And they all agreed they would.